Martin's Midnight Muddle

by David Clayton

Illustrated by Julie Anderson

Introduction

When Martin tells Emma that he is going on

a secret trip, she wonders what he is up to.

What is going on?

Emma and Debbie just have to find out.

Martin is always
messing things
up, but you have
to like him.
People get mad
with him, but he
thinks he's
perfect!

Emma, Martin's girlfriend, is

cool-headed and nice looking.

Nothing is out of place in her life

– except Martin!

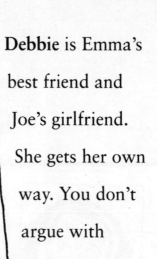

Debbie is Emma's best friend and Joe's girlfriend. She gets her own way. You don't argue with Debs!

Joe is easy-going. Hardly anyone gets him mad – apart from Martin!

Chapter 1

My boyfriend, Martin, is a nice lad. But he is always in a mess. Some people are like that, aren't they?

Last year, he took me to Blackpool. He had the tickets but then he lost them.

It took us *ten hours* to walk home. All we had to eat was one packet of mints!

AND nobody could come for us! You see, Dad's phone was dead and Martin isn't even on the phone!

My dad blew up when Martin told him about the tickets.

"Emma, that lad's a fool," Dad said when Martin had gone. "I don't know why you bother with him."

"He's fun," I said. "He cheers me up."

It was ages before Dad shut up about it.

But last week, Martin was at it again – doing things *his* way.

Emma, that lad's a fool.

Chapter 2

Right after school Martin broke the news to me. "I can't come out tonight. Me and Joe are doing something special."

"TONIGHT?" I said. "What about me and Debbie? It's Friday!"

The four of us always go out at weekends. On Friday, we go to the roller-disco. On Saturday, we go ten-pin bowling.

"You'll have to watch telly with Debs!" said Martin.

"You must be joking!" I said. "Stay in on a Friday? You can't dump us like that!

What are you up to?" I asked.

"Can't tell you. It's a secret."

"Are you meeting some other girls?"

"No, of course not. We just want to do something ... *new*."

And he was OFF! "Goodbye, Emma. See you Monday!" BANG! GONE!

I didn't like this at all! What was their game? I rang Debbie and told her about the trip.

"*What* did you say?" she said.

"They are going on a secret trip. Martin won't tell me where to," I said.

"I'll find out!" she snapped. "Joe will tell me. I'll make him! If it's another girl, he's *dead!*"

Chapter 3

Five minutes later, Debbie rang me back.

"They're going camping at Moor Top Farm. He *says*. But it seems odd to me. They never go off on their own! And he said we had to stay in. What is going on?"

"What are we going to do?" I asked.

"We are going up there. We'll find out what they're up to! Bring clothes and some food."

"What about a tent?"

"I've got one, and all the gear. Dad will

drive us there. See you at six. Don't tell

Martin!"

What a laugh! Good old Debbie!

Martin and Joe would get a surprise!

Chapter 4

Six o'clock came fast. Deb's dad came in his big black Range Rover.

Away we went. Out of the street. Out of the town. Past the park. Up and up and up the hills. Soon we were there – Moor Top. There was a pub, a post office, a school and a little field for camping. Soon, Deb's dad was gone. We quickly put our tent up.

There were lots of tents on the field. Big tents, small tents, posh tents, scruffy tents. But no sign of Martin's tent! You could not miss Martin's tent. It was green and yellow and messy. I had seen it in his garden. It was rubbish.

But it was not there.

"Where can they be?" I asked.

Debbie laughed. "Lost! What twits!"

It was a warm evening. We drank some coffee. We sang songs. We were camping. Boys or no boys!

"Shhh!!!" said Deb suddenly.

"What?"

"Look!"

Chapter 5

Two boys were coming on to the field.
Both had big packs on.

"OOOOOOOOO! MY FEET!" said
one of them.

"*Your* feet?" said the other. "YOU are
the one who lost the bus tickets! AND got
us put off the bus! Five miles we've had to
walk!"

Yes, Martin had done it again!

Deb looked at me. "Don't say
anything!" she whispered. "Let's have
some fun!"

The boys lay on the ground for a long time.

"We'll have to put the tent up soon. It's late already," said Joe.

"OK!" said Martin. He got out a hammer. "Give me the pegs."

"Here you are," said Joe.

"Oh no!" groaned Martin.

"What's the matter? The bag says 'pegs'."

"Yes," said Martin, "but these are *clothes* pegs for hanging up washing! We need *tent* pegs!"

Deb and I nearly burst out laughing. But we said nothing!

"We could still sleep in it," said Joe.

"Sleep in a flat tent? We'd be cold and wet!" Martin was *not* happy.

"I wish I was at the roller-disco!" Joe wasn't happy either.

"Don't be a wimp! Let's go and get a drink," said Martin.

Off they went to the pub.

Then we laughed!

Chapter 6

While the boys were gone, Debbie went over to their tent. She left a bag there.

A bit later the boys came back.

"Hey! Someone has given us some pegs!"

Martin got his hammer out again. Bang! Bang! Bang! In went the pegs. Up went two scruffy tents.

"Shut up, you lads!" Everybody around was shouting at them!

"Shall we tell them we are here?" I said.

"No," said Deb, "let's watch them.
They think they are ace, but they can't
camp at all!"

Chapter 7

Debbie was right!

We could hear everything the boys said.

"I'm very hungry!" said Joe. "Let's make something to eat."

"Isn't there a chip shop here?" said Martin. "I can't cook."

"Well, I can't cook either!" Joe sounded fed up.

"It isn't hard. Even Emma can do it!" Martin laughed.

Oh! Even Emma can do it, eh? I stood up. I was going to go over and bop him!

Deb stopped me. "No! Shh! This is great! We can watch them make a mess of it!"

Martin was going to show Joe how to cook.

"First, you light the stove."

"Yes."

"Then, you put the food in the pan."

Joe shook his head.

"But where is the food?"

Martin laughed.

"Don't be silly! It's in the tins!"

"So, how do we get it out?"

"With the tin-opener ..."

"So where's that? I'm hungry. Come on!"

"Ah!" said Martin after looking in his pack.

"Yes?"

"Well, we haven't GOT one! But I've got a pen knife."

Deb and I were laughing so hard we almost fell over. No pegs! No tin-opener!

Chapter 8

Now Joe was mad.

"I'm fed up with you, Martin. You got us thrown off the bus, and now there's no tin-opener! We can't eat *grass*!"

Suddenly Martin was shouting. "Hey! Look at that! FIRE! Come on!"

A FIRE! Were they on fire? That wasn't a laugh!

But no! The family tent next to them was on fire.

A child was crying. The side of the tent was orange with flames.

Martin was over in a flash. Up went
the zip. In he went.

"Be careful, Martin!" I yelled.

We dashed over.

WHOOOOOOF!!!!

Now it really went up!

Martin had been gone for ages. Then there he was. He was sliding along the grass. He dragged a little kid of about two with him.

Chapter 9

The whole camp was around Martin. The baby's mum and dad were crying.

"We only went to phone!" they said.

"Martin!" I cried. "Are you hurt?"

"Emma!" He was surprised to see me. "I'm all right."

"That was very brave, son!" said the farmer.

"Hey! What are you two doing here? We haven't even phoned yet!" said Joe.

"What do you mean *phoned*?" I said.

"That's why we're here," Joe said.

"It's a surprise for you two," added
Martin. "We were going to set up a tent
for you. Then phone you up."

"OH YES?" I said.

"Yes, look!" he pointed. "That's why
we put up *two* tents."

"AND we were going to make some
food for you," said Joe. "We've got loads
of tins. Two lots – one for us, one for you
and Debbie!"

"Well, you'll need this then!" I gave
him the tin-opener. "But we don't need
your food. Debbie brought ours ..."

"No!" said Debbie. "*You* were going to
bring the food."

My face went red!

"Oh no!" I groaned. "I've left it in
your dad's car!"

"I knew it would all work out all right in the end!" said Martin. "My tins, your opener! What a team!"

I had to laugh! I felt such a fool!

"Don't worry!" Martin went on. "We're ace at camping, aren't we, Joe?"

Then we really had a laugh. It was nearly midnight before we got everything sorted out. Good old Martin – the master of muck-ups – had done something right at last!